The Colors We Eat

White Foods

Patricia Whitehouse

Heinemann Library

Chicago, Illinois

Customer Service 888-454-2279
Visit our website at www.heinemannlibrary.com

Designed by Sue Emerson, Heinemann Library
Printed and bound in the U.S.A. by Lake Book

06 05 04 03 02
10 9 8 7 6 5 4 3 2 1

Library of Congress Cataloging-in-Publication Data
Whitehouse, Patricia, 1958-
    White foods / Patricia Whitehouse.
        p. cm. — (The colors we eat)
Includes index.
Summary: Introduces things to eat and drink that are white, from rice to milk.
    ISBN: 1-58810-538-5 (HC), 1-58810-746-9 (Pbk.)
    1. Food—Juvenile literature. 2. White—Juvenile literature. [1. Food. 2. White.] I. Title
II. Series
    TX355.W482 2002
    641.3—dc21

                    2001006289

Acknowledgments
The author and publishers are grateful to the following for permission to reproduce copyright material:
Title page, pp. 4, 5, 6, 7L, 7R, 8, 9, 10, 12, 13, 14, 15, 16, 17, 19 Michael Brosilow/Heinemann Library; p. 11
Greg Beck/Fraser Photos; p. 18 Amor Montes de Oca; pp. 20, 21L, 21R Craig Mitchelldyer Photography

Cover photograph by Michael Brosilow/Heinemann Library

Every effort has been made to contact copyright holders of any material reproduced in this book.
Any omissions will be rectified in subsequent printings if notice is given to the publisher.

Special thanks to our advisory panel for their help in the preparation of this book:
Eileen Day, Preschool Teacher
Chicago, IL

Paula Fischer, K–1 Teacher
Indianapolis, IN

Sandra Gilbert,
Library Media Specialist
Houston, TX

Angela Leeper,
Educational Consultant
North Carolina Department
of Public Instruction
Raleigh, NC

Pam McDonald, Reading Teacher
Winter Springs, FL

Melinda Murphy,
Library Media Specialist
Houston, TX

Helen Rosenberg, MLS
Chicago, IL

Anna Marie Varakin,
Reading Instructor
Western Maryland College

Some words are shown in bold, **like this.**
You can find them in the picture glossary on page 23.

Contents

Have You Eaten White Foods?

Colors are all around you.

You might have eaten some of these colors.

There are white fruits and vegetables.

There are other white foods, too.

What Are Some Big White Foods?

Cauliflower is big and white.

It is the flowers of a cauliflower plant.

This loaf of bread is big and white.

Bread is made from **flour**.

What Are Some Other Big White Foods?

Turnips are big and white.

The white part grows under the ground.

This onion is big and white.

The white part grows under
the ground, too.

What Are Some Small White Foods?

Bean sprouts are small and white.

Sprouts are plants that just began growing.

Popcorn is small and white.

Popcorn **kernels** have to be hot before they pop.

What Are Some Other Small White Foods?

Rice is small and white.

Rice has to be cooked so it is soft enough to eat.

These eggs are small and white.

Most white eggs come from chickens.

What Are Some Crunchy White Foods?

Macadamia nuts are crunchy and white.

They are the seeds of a macadamia tree.

Jicama is crunchy and white.

We eat the root of the jicama plant.

What Are Some Soft White Foods?

This **cottage cheese** is soft and white.

It is made from milk.

Mashed potatoes are soft and white.

They are made with cooked potatoes.

What White Foods Can You Drink?

Milk is white.

Most milk we drink comes from cows.

Potato soup is white.

It is made with potatoes and milk.

White Sundae Recipe

Ask an adult to help you.

First, spoon vanilla yogurt into a cup.

Sprinkle some coconut on the yogurt.

Next, squirt in some whipped cream.

Add more layers until the cup is full.

Then eat your white sundae!

Quiz

Can you name these white foods?

Look for the answers on page 24.

Picture Glossary

bean sprouts
page 10

jicama
(HIC-ah-ma)
page 15

cauliflower
page 6

kernels
page 11

cottage cheese
page 16

macadamia nuts
(mack-uh-DAY-mee-uh nuts)
page 14

flour
page 7

turnip
page 8

23

Note to Parents and Teachers

Reading for information is an important part of a child's literacy development. Learning begins with a question about something. Help children think of themselves as investigators and researchers by encouraging their questions about the world around them. Each chapter in this book begins with a question. Read the question together. Look at the pictures. Talk about what you think the answer might be. Then read the text to find out if your predictions were correct. Think of other questions you could ask about the topic, and discuss where you might find the answers. Assist children in using the picture glossary and the index to practice new vocabulary and research skills.

Index

Answers to quiz on page 22

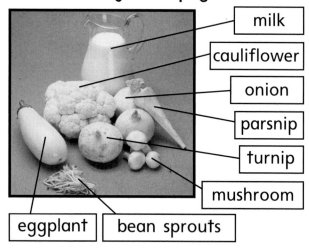

milk

cauliflower

onion

parsnip

turnip

mushroom

eggplant   bean sprouts